MiA MAYHEM

#8

STEALS THE SHOW!

BY **KARA WEST**   ILLUSTRATED BY **LEEZA HERNANDEZ**

LITTLE SIMON

New York   London   Toronto   Sydney   New Delhi

LITTLE SIMON
An imprint of Simon & Schuster Children's Publishing Division
1230 Avenue of the Americas, New York, New York 10020
First Little Simon paperback edition July 2020
Copyright © 2020 by Simon & Schuster, Inc.
Also available in a Little Simon hardcover edition
All rights reserved, including the right of reproduction in whole or in part in any form.
LITTLE SIMON is a registered trademark of Simon & Schuster, Inc., and associated colophon is a trademark of Simon & Schuster, Inc.
For information about special discounts for bulk purchases, please contact Simon & Schuster Special Sales at 1-866-506-1949 or business@simonandschuster.com.
The Simon & Schuster Speakers Bureau can bring authors to your live event. For more information or to book an event contact the Simon & Schuster Speakers Bureau at 1-866-248-3049 or visit our website at www.simonspeakers.com.
Designed by Laura Roode
Manufactured in the United States of America 0920 BVG
2 4 6 8 10 9 7 5 3
This book has been cataloged with the Library of Congress.
ISBN 978-1-5344-6724-8 (hc)
ISBN 978-1-5344-6723-1 (pbk)
ISBN 978-1-5344-6725-5 (eBook)

CONTENTS

How to Be a Good Superhero

I'm going to be a star!

Okay, maybe not *immediately*. First I'm going to ace this audition. *Then* I'm going to be a star.

I'm in my theater class, and I can't wait to get up onstage!

I've been preparing for this day ever since our teacher, Ms. Montgomery, announced the school play.

This year's show is called *How to Be a Good Superhero*.

And guess who happens to be one in real life?

Believe it or not . . . *me*!

Like for real!

My name is Mia  Macarooney, and *I. Am. A. Superhero!*

Now, I know I don't look very super right now. When I'm at Normal Elementary School, I'm just a regular kid.

But after this audition is over, I'm going straight to another school called the Program for In Training Superheroes, aka the PITS! And at *that* place, I go by my superhero name—Mia Mayhem! I've learned how to use all kinds of awesome powers. But really, the most important part of my training has been learning how to be a good superhero.

So that's why I know I'm perfect for this play!

After a group of my classmates performed, Ms. Montgomery finally called my name. My best friend, Eddie Stein, gave me a big thumbs-up.

"Break a leg!" he whispered. "But obviously, not for real."

He was my only friend in the entire world who knew my super-secret. And he also knew how excited I was for this moment.

I got up, ready to impress everyone.
But as I walked onto the stage,
something strange happened.
My mind went totally blank.

I looked out in horror as my whole class stared back at me. And that wasn't even the worst part.

Forgetting my *lines* was one thing, but I suddenly forgot how to *talk*, *too*!

I opened my mouth, but nothing came out.

It was only after Ms. Montgomery recited a scene with me that I started to remember.

After a long, awkward silence, I mumbled through the scene, skipping over most of what I had prepared.

Just a few minutes ago, I felt like I was on top of the world. But now I was living my worst nightmare.

And all I wanted to do was get off that stage.

CHAPTER 2

TREE TIME

After everyone else performed, we waited in the student lounge while Ms. Montgomery cast the roles. I paced back and forth in a corner, not wanting to talk to anyone.

But soon it was the moment of truth. My teacher walked in and tacked the cast list onto the student bulletin board.

I was sure that my name wouldn't even be on it. But it turns out that my name was on the list, all right.

Not as a superhero . . . but as a *tree*! Can you believe it?

CAST LIST

SUPERHERO: BAILEY

RACCOON: DAISY

DOG: HENRY

MOUSE: SOPHIE

BAD GUY: ZACK

STAGE DESIGN: EDDIE

TREE: MIA

I know I just had the most terrible audition *ever*, but I was definitely *not* happy. After all, who wants to be a tree in a play about *superheroes*?

"Maybe it'll be a *talking* tree!" Eddie said cheerfully.

I knew I could always count on Eddie to look on the bright side.

I wanted to be as excited about the play as he was, but that was easier for him. Eddie got the exact role he wanted: costume and stage designer!

Eddie happily talked about some of the ideas he had, and I nodded along.

But it was hard to focus. The truth was that even though I knew it was just a play, in a weird way, it felt like I had failed at being myself!

So when Ms. Montgomery finally handed out the script, I hoped Eddie was right. Maybe in this superhero world, trees could really talk!

I eagerly flipped through the whole play.

On every single page, there were stage directions that said SUPERHERO IN FRONT OF TREE or ANIMAL NEXT TO TREE.

But the tree itself?

It said nothing.

I had zero lines.

But here's the catch: The tree was in *every* scene!

Normally I would be excited about this, but now I wasn't so sure.

"At least you'll get to be a part of every rehearsal," Eddie said as we left class. "You'll be the best tree this school has ever seen!"

"Yeah, I guess so. Thanks, Eddie," I replied, still a bit bummed. "How many tree roles do you think there have been?"

"Hmm, at least . . . *tree*?" he joked, holding up three fingers. "Get it? Tree? Three?"

It was a *terrible* joke, but it did make me smile. Eddie was the *bestest* friend in the world. I gave him a big hug, and then we said good-bye.

I may not have been very good at acting onstage, but luckily, it was time to be super for real—as the one and only MIA MAYHEM!

THE OBSERVATION DECK

At the front door of the PITS, I quick-changed into my supersuit. Then I turned the crooked DO NOT ENTER sign, and a hidden screen popped up and then scanned my face.

From the outside the PITS looked like an old abandoned warehouse, but on the inside it was a top secret superhero training academy!

The lobby, known as the Compass, was already bustling with superheroes.

I took the elevator to the second floor, where all the junior level classes were held. Then I walked into a gym that had large thunderbolt-shaped windows in the inner walls.

I went up to the closest one and saw a group of fifth-year students warming up down below. This wasn't any old gym—it had an observation deck!

On the ground floor, I saw that there was one entire wall that was made up of small rectangular drawers. To get the best view, I grabbed a seat in the front row of the bleachers as someone called my name.

"Hey, Mia!" my friend Allie Oomph called.

Right behind her were our other two friends, Penn Powers and Ben Ocular. Ben's adorable guide dog and sidekick, Seeker, was there too.

"So how was the audition?" Penn asked.

"I bet you were a smash hit!" Allie chimed in.

I suddenly wished I hadn't told them about the play. I had been so excited about it that I'd been talking about it for weeks.

"Ugh," I groaned. "Don't even get me started."

I took a deep breath, not wanting to relive that moment. And thankfully, Dr. Sue Perb, the school's headmistress, walked into the room before I had to say more.

"Welcome to the PITS Escape Room Observation Deck!" she announced. "As you know, a good superhero must be aware of what's going on around them at all times. That is why *super-focus* and *teamwork* will be the keys to solving today's mission."

The group of fifth-year students who had been warming up earlier were going to show us a demo. As soon as an alarm went off, the superheroes got down to business.

They split into pairs and quickly

solved a bunch of riddles that appeared on a giant screen near the ceiling. I couldn't believe how well they worked under pressure. I hoped that watching them would help me feel as ready . . . but it didn't help one bit.

And before I knew it, it was our turn. Thankfully, Allie, Penn, Ben, and Seeker were on my team.

We waited while the red numbers on the clock counted down to zero.

"Hey, guys! We can do this!" Allie yelled out as she gave everyone a high five.

I was glad that Allie was confident. But as the seconds ticked down, I just hoped that I wouldn't freeze up.

CHAPTER 4

Locked in the Escape Room

Down on the first floor, the escape room looked much bigger than it had when we were above it.

The first wall was lined with rows and rows of small rectangular drawers.

The second wall had the countdown clock, while the third one had the large screen near the ceiling.

The fourth wall was bare.

The door the older students had just escaped from had disappeared.

When the timer began, our first instructions appeared on-screen. It read: "There is only one way out. You must find the hidden door."

"Let's try our powers first," Allie said.

THERE IS ONLY ONE WAY OUT. YOU MUST FIND THE HIDDEN DOOR.

TICK TICK TICK TICK TICK TICK

"Mia, do you want to come give me a hand?"

I nodded and then walked over to the empty wall. On the count of three, we pushed with all our might, hoping we could break through it.

It did *not* work.

"Wow, this wall must be made with some super-duper, extra-heavy stuff," Allie said, panting.

Right then, Penn pushed off the ground to fly over to us. But instead of lifting up, he hovered above the floor for a second before landing again.

"Hey! I can't fly!" he exclaimed. "I don't think it's the wall. Our superpowers don't work in here."

Just to be sure, we tried using every single power we knew how to use. Allie tried to run. Ben tried to x-ray through the wall. And I kept pushing. But Penn was right! Nothing worked.

"What do we do now?" Allie asked after we all gave up.

"Hey, guys! Look at the screen!" Penn said.

The digits 1-5-0 had popped up.

"There are also numbers on the drawers," Allie replied. "The screen is telling us which one to open first!"

The only problem was that these drawers were not in numerical order.

I glanced at the clock. We only had ten minutes left, so we needed to act fast.

"Guys, we don't have time!" I cried.

I pulled open the drawer closest to me. But that was a bad idea . . . because we all immediately got smacked with banana cream pies.

I felt so bad that I decided that it'd be best if I just stayed out of the way. Luckily, not long after, Allie and Ben found the right numbered drawer.

Inside, there was a series of riddles we had to solve.

As I watched from the corner, I was impressed by how many answers my friends knew. If I was locked in here by myself, I would have never stood a chance.

Then, with thirty seconds left, my friends rushed over to the other side of the room to open the last drawer. But right when they turned around, they slipped on the banana cream pies on the floor!

So just like that, we were the only team that had run out of time.

And of course, it was all my fault.

CHAPTER 5

Who's the Real Superhero?

"Okay, almost done," Ms. Montgomery said.

I was standing with my arms straight out as she measured me for my tree costume at rehearsal the next day.

"Mia, this is going to look great!" Eddie said excitedly as he wrote down the measurements Ms. Montgomery called out.

I still didn't *want* to be a tree. But after causing a pie disaster at the PITS, it was probably safer to be a tree than to be myself. Plus, if I *had* to wear a tree costume, at least Eddie was going to make it look cool.

As soon as they finished, Ms. Montgomery moved on to the next kid.

"How was yesterday at the PITS?" Eddie whispered as soon as our teacher walked away.

"Absolute mayhem," I said, looking down at my feet. I could still taste the banana cream pie. "We had an escape room mission, but I got so nervous watching the clock that I wasn't much help. We were the only team that didn't make it out!"

"Oh," said Eddie. "That's okay."

"No, it was all my fault!" I cried as I explained what happened with the pies.

Eddie patted me on the back and smiled. I thanked him and then walked onstage to my spot. Being a tree shouldn't be hard. The only thing I needed to do was stand still and stay out of the way.

The star of our show was my classmate Bailey Brightman, and I had to admit that she was a pretty great superhero. I watched as she ran, jumped, and tumbled across the stage. She was definitely good, but secretly, I wished I were having as much fun as her.

Then at one point Bailey almost tripped over her long cape. But somehow, she steadied herself and continued on as if nothing had happened!

If that had been me, I would have forgotten my line, tripped over my cape, and made everyone else fall too.

You see, the thing is, I have a pretty long history of causing mayhem. One time I broke a goalpost while playing soccer, and another time, I broke a water fountain!

SPLOOSH!

Yeah, the more I thought about it, it was a good thing I was a tree.

And as rehearsal went on, being a tree was actually pretty fun. I had the best front row seat to all the action!

So by the end of class, I was in a much better mood.

Eddie and I walked over to his house after rehearsal, and I watched as he began to make my costume. Junior, Eddie's personal robot, was helping him. Junior was a very friendly robot (as long as he didn't grow *too* big—literally!), and they made an awesome team.

"Mia, I know you're not that excited to be a tree, but . . . ," Eddie started as he cut out a large branch.

"Oh, don't worry, Eddie," I said with a smile. "I think it's a good thing I'm a tree. It's not dangerous."

Eddie nodded and gave me a big thumbs-up.

I have to admit that as a real superhero, it felt weird to be avoiding anything dangerous, but for now, I needed to learn how to relax.

If I could do that, I had a good feeling things would be okay.

READY . . . SET . . . ACTION!

And guess what?

I was right!

Once I decided that I really was going to be the best cardboard tree there ever was, rehearsal got a lot better.

From my spot at the back of the stage (or "upstage," as Ms. Montgomery called it), I could see *everything*.

I might not have any lines, but I was onstage more than anybody else, *even* Bailey. And *that* was . . . pretty cool!

Not only that, but as I watched every scene, I ended up learning every

single part! So sometimes I secretly helped classmates remember their lines. I loved knowing and feeling in control of every scene, even if I wasn't acting in it.

I watched as Bailey learned how to roll, jump, and glide as she saved a bunch of kids from a moving train. Watching the action scenes were the only times I wished I could jump in.

But being a tree definitely had its perks. When it was time for the moving train to exit the stage, the kids didn't know where to go. So I quickly pointed over at the *x* mark on the floor.

Then in the next scene, a stuffed animal kitten was stuck up in a tree. Or I guess it was stuck to *me* . . . since I *was* the tree!

All throughout the scene, I tried my best not to laugh.

But it wasn't easy.

I watched as Ms. Montgomery hooked Bailey up to a bunch of wires. So far, we'd been practicing without them, but now it was time to learn how to fly!

I couldn't wait to see how this was going to work!

Bailey stood still as Ms. Montgomery attached the wires. I was impressed because she looked totally calm and cool. But then our teacher pushed the button on the lifting machine. When Bailey lifted into the air, her face went as white as a ghost.

CLICK!

She wasn't that high up, but I could see what nobody else could: Bailey was scared! Really, really scared!

"Mia, I feel like I'm going to fall!" Bailey whispered down to me in a panic.

Although Bailey didn't know why, I knew exactly how she felt.

"Don't worry. Just look straight ahead," I said with a smile. "And take a deep breath."

She nodded and then slowly looked up. I could tell that she was trying her hardest to be brave. When her feet landed back on the ground a few minutes later, her whole body was shaking.

I held out a hand to help steady her.

"Thanks," she said. Then she took a big breath. "Hey, Mia?"

"Yeah?"

"I don't think I can do this!"

PRACTICE MAKES PERFECT

I felt terrible for Bailey.

Being a real superhero, I totally understood how scary heights could feel.

It wasn't that long ago that I got stuck at the top of a *very* high climbing rope because I was afraid to look down! That happened during my superhero placement exam on my first day at the PITS!

"You *can* do this. You just need to practice to get over your fear and feel more comfortable," I said. "I can help you!"

I could tell she didn't believe me, but she nodded gratefully.

"Thanks, Mia," she replied.

"No sweat," I said as I gave her a big thumbs-up.

Knowing that I could help Bailey instantly made me feel confident about my own super-skills. Just like I had told Bailey, patience and practice were the key to staying relaxed under pressure.

After rehearsal I headed to the PITS
knowing exactly what I needed to do.
It was going to be our second chance
at the escape room, and I was feeling
more prepared than ever.

I joined my friends in the same room with the wall of drawers.

Right before the alarm was about to go off, I looked over at Penn, Allie, Ben, and Seeker.

"Guys, I'm sorry about the banana pies," I said. "I know we can find our way out of here."

"Oh, Mia. No need to be sorry!" said Allie. "It wasn't just you. None of us worked together!"

"You're right. We need to be a team," Ben said.

I nodded in agreement.

Then I reminded myself that staying relaxed under pressure was the key.

And this time things felt totally different. We were patient. We listened to one another and followed the clues. And thanks to our awesome teamwork, we breezed through every riddle.

In fact, things went even better than we hoped because in the end, we didn't just *beat* the time—we set a new PITS record! Finding the hidden door taught me that practice and patience would help me beat anything.

So the next morning I told Ms. Montgomery that I would work with Bailey on the wires. I decided that the best way to help was for us to do it together. Since Eddie was the only one who knew I could fly for real, I let my teacher secure the wires to my harness. And then Bailey and I lifted into the air!

At first Bailey didn't like it. But each day I pushed her a little bit more. And every day she got better and better.

Then by our last rehearsal, Bailey was gliding near the top of the ceiling!

I got ready to give her a big high five as she came down.

But the minute I saw her, I knew something was wrong. She looked like she was going to throw up any minute.

"Oh no, Bailey, you have a fever," Ms. Montgomery said as she felt Bailey's forehead.

So our teacher sent her to the nurse, and then Bailey went home to rest.

I couldn't believe it.

Just like that, our superhero was out of commission, and the whole play was now in danger!

CHAPTER
8

THE UNEXPECTED UNDERSTUDY

As expected, Bailey didn't come to school the next day. Ms. Montgomery told us Bailey had a really bad stomach bug.

I knew how that felt, and it was no fun—at all.

We were gathered in the theater, and everybody looked so disappointed. Of course, it wasn't Bailey's fault . . . but without her, we couldn't do the show!

"I'm sorry, everyone," said Ms. Montgomery. "If we had an understudy who had been practicing Bailey's role, we'd be okay. But because we don't, I'm afraid we're going to have to cancel the opening night. The good news is that she should be better for tomorrow's show."

Everybody groaned.

"You've all worked so hard," she said sadly. "But this superhero play is missing a superhero!"

And that's when Eddie raised his hand. "I have an idea!" he cried.

"Yes, what is it, Eddie?" asked Ms. Montgomery.

"You know, there *is* someone here who has been to every single rehearsal," he said. "*And* she knows every line."

Then he turned around and smiled
right at me.

"What?" I squeaked. *"Me?"*

"Yes, you!" he said, beaming with a
huge grin. "I know you can do it!"

"No, I don't think that's a good
idea," I said quickly. "I was too nervous
to even finish my audition!"

But to my surprise, everyone was nodding and smiling at me. Even Ms. Montgomery seemed to love the idea.

"I can't do it," I said, shaking my head.

"Mia, come on!" Eddie begged. "You know *all* the lines and can handle *all* the action! I know you'd make a *very* good superhero." He smiled at me again with a twinkle in his eye.

I looked back at my friend and then at everyone else.

I still really didn't like the idea.

But I hated the idea of canceling the show even more.

So I took a deep breath and decided to trust my gut.

"Well . . . ," I said slowly, trying to ignore the growing butterflies in my stomach. "Okay, I'll give it a try!"

We only had an hour of rehearsal left, and I had to learn Bailey's entire part. The funny thing was that Eddie was totally right! I knew every single line, and I was totally prepared for this!

At the end of rehearsal, I was feeling great—until Ms. Montgomery pointed out one very big problem.

She held up Bailey's costume.

Bailey was taller
than I was, and there
was *no* way that
costume would
fit me! I tried it
on, just to be
sure, but I
did not look
very heroic.

At all.

I changed back to my regular clothes, bummed that I wouldn't be able to wear the costume that Eddie helped make.

But luckily, I knew I had the perfect solution.

CHAPTER 9

THE SHOW MUST GO ON!

That's how I ended up wearing my very own supersuit, in front of the whole school, *pretending* to be a superhero!

I couldn't believe it. Maybe it was the practice, or maybe it was because I was wearing my own suit, but I felt totally cool!

And you know what? I was actually good at this acting thing!

Now that I knew all the lines and where to go, my nerves went away, and I was having a blast!

Of course, not a *real* blast, though. There were no explosions needed for this play.

The only thing I needed to worry about was taking things easy. I didn't want to put my fist through the stage props or make the wires break by mistake, after all. In a weird way, for me, pretending to be a superhero turned out to be almost harder than being a real one!

But thankfully, I made it through the runaway train scene without any major hiccups. And soon, it was time to rescue the kitten. I ran up to the tree and smiled at my replacement—my best friend, Eddie!

I'd volunteered him to be the tree, and he happily took my spot.

We nodded at each other before I went up in the air with the wires attached. I was very careful to not use my actual flying skills because that would have given my secret away . . . but I might have added a few extra flips for some super-flair.

Then I rescued the cat and said my last line as the big red stage curtains closed. When they opened back up, the entire cast took a bow, and the crowd erupted in applause.

I couldn't believe how fast the show had gone. Back when I had my terrible audition, it was like time had completely stopped. But now that I was enjoying myself, time seemed to fly!

We all walked to the edge of the
stage to take our bows one more time.
I looked out into the audience where
my mom and dad were.

I gave them a wink as my dad
whistled with his fingers.

Being onstage felt incredible.

I knew I was a pretty good real
superhero. And after today, it turned
out that I could be a pretty good
pretend one, too!

CHAPTER 10

EXIT

BRAVA!

In the dressing room, the entire cast celebrated the night.

Eddie came over and gave me a huge hug. And Ms. Montgomery did too.

"Mia absolutely saved the day," she gushed to my mom and dad, who had come backstage. "If it hadn't been for her, we wouldn't have had a play at all!"

"Oh, she *does* tend to save the day,"
Dad said with a smile.

"And we couldn't be prouder," said
Mom. "Brava!"

"Yes, Mia. Great job! And it looks like you've got some awesome fans!" Dad said as he handed me a big bouquet of flowers.

I found a card wedged between the flowers.

It read:

To Mia Macarooney,
Thanks for saving the play tonight. You'll be SUPER!
Love,
Bailey Brightman

I knew that Bailey had worked so hard for the role, so it was extra sweet of her to send me flowers.

Then my parents left while I changed back into my regular clothes. It was only then that I found another bouquet waiting for me at my spot by the mirror.

I opened another letter that read:

To Mia Mayhem
you're our SUPERSTAR!
Love,
Mom + Dad
x

I smiled big as I read their card. Even though only three people knew, I'd had fun being onstage as MIA MAYHEM for the first and probably last time ever.

I looked at myself in the mirror. For the first time that night, my happy nerves were gone and I could finally take it all in.

This definitely wasn't how I expected the evening to end, but it turns out that I *was* the perfect fit for the play.

Through this show, I learned that no matter where I am—at regular school or at the PITS—I'll always be both Mia Macarooney AND Mia Mayhem!

After all, it takes both parts for me to be exactly who I am.

And that's why when Bailey comes back for the final show tomorrow, I think I'll be more than happy to be a regular old tree.

DON'T MISS MIA MAYHEM'S NEXT ADVENTURE!

Ever get that funny déjà vu feeling when you know you've totally seen something or been somewhere before?

Well, I just had it!

I opened my mailbox today, and right on top was an envelope covered in stamps. I got goose bumps because it looked exactly like an old letter I got that changed my whole life!

You see, I was regular Mia Macarooney until the day a very similar-looking letter arrived. On that day, I found out that I was actually super! Like for real! *I. Am. A. Superhero!*

And long story short, my superhero name is Mia Mayhem! I still have a lot to learn, so I go to a top secret training academy every day after regular school called the Program for In Training Superheroes, aka the PITS!

So obviously I thought this letter was for me . . . until I looked down and saw it was for my parents! I ran inside as fast as I could to deliver the mysterious letter.

"Mom! Dad!" I gasped as I tried to catch my breath. I had rushed into the kitchen so fast that I bumped right into my dad, knocking over a bowl of Cheez Bytes.

Oops!

I would normally clean up right away, but this was more important.

I handed the letter to my mom, who had crackers all over her hair, and eagerly waited for her to open it.